Library and Archives Canada Cataloguing in Publication

Cole, Kathryn, author
A tattle-tell tale : a story about getting help / written by
Kathryn Cole ; illustrated by Qin Leng.

(I'm a great little kid series)
Co-published by: Boost Child & Youth Advocacy Centre.
ISBN 978-1-927583-92-0 (hardback)

1. Bullying in schools—Juvenile fiction. 2. Communication—Juvenile fiction.
I. Leng, Qin, illustrator II. Boost Child & Youth Advocacy Centre, sponsoring body III. Title.

PS8605.O4353T37 2016   jC813'.6   C2015-908363-X

*Boost Child & Youth Advocacy Centre gratefully acknowledges the generous support
of Rogers Communications for funding the development and publication of the Prevention
Program Series. Rogers Communications is an important partner in our efforts to prevent
abuse and violence in children's lives.*

*Second Story Press gratefully acknowledges the support of the Ontario Arts Council and the
Canada Council for the Arts for our publishing program. We acknowledge the financial support
of the Government of Canada through the Canada Book Fund.*

ONTARIO ARTS COUNCIL
CONSEIL DES ARTS DE L'ONTARIO
an Ontario government agency
un organisme du gouvernement de l'Ontario

Canada Council   Conseil des Arts
for the Arts   du Canada

Funded by the Government of Canada
Financé par le gouvernement du Canada

Canada

Published by
Second Story Press
20 Maud Street, Suite 401
Toronto, Ontario, Canada
M5V 2M5
www.secondstorypress.ca

A Tattle-tell Tale

A story about getting help

written by Kathryn Cole
illustrated by Qin Leng

Second Story Press

Joseph was hungry. His mom had packed an egg salad sandwich – his favorite – and a brownie for dessert. He was about to take a bite of the sandwich when a big kid from grade seven walked past his table.

"It's Martin!" whispered Devon. "Quick. Hide your dessert! He always grabs something."

"Let's see what you little kids have for me today," Martin said, looking over the food.

Joseph tried to cover his brownie with his arm, but it was too late.

"Big mistake, Kid. I saw that. Gimme the brownie."

Joseph was afraid to say no. He handed over the brownie. His friends at the table said nothing, but Joseph was upset that he hadn't stood up for himself.

That was on Monday.

On Tuesday at lunchtime, Martin came back. He went straight to Joseph. "What's for dessert today, Kid?" he asked.

Joseph reluctantly showed him the three chocolate chip cookies he was saving.

"Not bad," Martin said. "Oh! And lookee here! A salami and cheese sandwich! Give it to me. You can keep the carrots." Martin walked away with most of Joseph's lunch.

Devon gave Joseph some celery to go with the carrots. And that's how Tuesday went.

The next day Joseph decided to eat in the boys' washroom, instead of the lunchroom. He didn't want to lose another lunch. Before he could start, the door flew open.

"I thought I saw you come in here. Did you think you could hide from me?" Martin grabbed Joseph's lunch bag and held it up high.

"Give it back!" Joseph demanded. "Or I'll…I'll…"

The bully laughed. "Or you'll do what?"

Joseph was afraid, but he was also angry. He put his head down and ran straight at Martin. Before he knew it, Joseph was on the bathroom floor and Martin was leaving with his lunch. "You'll be sorry if you tattle," he said.

On Wednesday Joseph went home hungry – with a headache.

On Thursday, Joseph asked Kamal to go with him to the washroom. He did, but when Martin showed up, Kamal ran. Joseph ran too, and ate his lunch at the far end of the schoolyard.

"Why are you eating out here, Joseph?" asked the yard-duty teacher.

Joseph gathered up his courage. Maybe he wouldn't be sorry if he told. Telling might be better than eating by himself. He just wouldn't name Martin. "I don't like to be bothered while I have my lunch," he told her. "And someone—"

Just then a girl fell and hurt her knee. The teacher hurried away to help. "Sorry, Joseph!" she called over her shoulder. "Enjoy your alone time."

Joseph didn't enjoy his alone time. He felt very...*alone*.

By afternoon recess, Joseph couldn't think about anything else. He had a BIG problem. He needed help, but how could he get it? Telling the yard-duty teacher hadn't worked. Who could he go to? His mom? His teacher? His classmates?

His mom was at work – he needed someone here. His teacher was sick today, and Joseph didn't know the supply teacher. His classmates were too afraid to help, even if they wanted to. Then he had an idea. He would get help from Mr. Tate without tattling. Mr. Tate always said the kids could come to him anytime.

Joseph tapped on the principal's door.

Mr. Tate opened his door and invited Joseph in. Joseph took a deep breath. "Do you have an extra key to the supply room, Mr. Tate? I was wondering if I could use it at lunchtime for a week or so…. Please."

Mr. Tate was very kind, but the answer was no. "Joseph," he said, "it might be better to tell me *why* you want to do that. You must have a good reason."

It was hard to begin, but telling the story got easier as Joseph went along. Mr. Tate listened carefully. "Do you know this boy's name?" he asked.

"It's Martin, but he told me I'd be sorry if I tattled."

Mr. Tate sat forward. "Joseph, there's a big difference between tattling and telling. When we tattle, we're trying to get someone into trouble. But we tell so we can get help. The important thing to remember is that someone needs help. This time, that someone is you. Do you understand?"

"I think so," Joseph answered. "But I still can't eat in the lunchroom or use the boys' bathroom."

Mr. Tate smiled. "Yes, you can. School should be a safe place for everyone, and it's my job to see that it is."

"But—" Joseph began.

"Don't worry. You were right to tell the whole story. Why don't I take a little tour of the lunchroom tomorrow? Martin doesn't have to know why I'm there," Mr. Tate said, as he showed Joseph out.

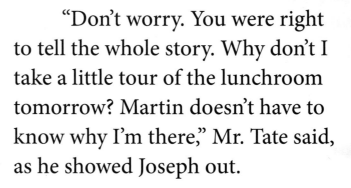

Thursday had been a long day. Even so, Joseph felt much better. He had shared his problem, and he trusted Mr. Tate to help.

On Friday at noon, Joseph went to eat in the lunchroom as Mr. Tate had said he should. Sure enough, Martin was there, waiting to pick on him.

"Hey, Kid. You got away from me yesterday." Martin came toward Joseph. "You better have something extra good for me today."

Joseph shuffled backwards.

"Oh, no you don't. You can run, but you can't hide."

At the very same time, the lunchroom door opened, and in stepped Mr. Tate. "Why would Joseph want to run and hide, Martin? Can you explain?"

The bully gasped. Standing next to Mr. Tate, Martin didn't look so big and scary.

Mr. Tate turned to Joseph. "Sit down and enjoy your lunch, Joseph. Martin and I are going to eat in my office and find a way to make things better for everyone. You have a good day, now."

On Friday Joseph had a *very* good day.

For Grown-ups

About Getting Help

How and where to get help involves recognizing and reaching out to people who can provide support and encouragement. A support system may include teachers, doctors, nurses, counselors, and police as well as family, friends, relatives, and neighbors. Trusting your feelings is important and that can guide you when deciding to seek help for yourself and others. The benefits of getting help are that you feel better and begin to trust and build confidence in yourself. Seeking the help you need, no matter how many times you have to ask, can help to resolve the problem.

Parents can support their children so that they feel comfortable in asking for help:

- **Identify supports**: Talk with children to identify who they would go to for help, recognizing that who they choose must be someone they trust.

- **Talk about secrets**: Discuss the difference between secrets and surprises – reinforce the message that no one should tell them to keep a secret about any kind of touch.

- **Always trust your feelings**: Emphasize to children that they should trust their feelings and talk to someone if they need help, even if they feel embarrassed, confused, or scared about telling.

- **Set an example**: Show children the different ways in which friends and family help one another.

- **Keep telling**: Empower children to get help for themselves and others by encouraging them to keep telling until someone helps them.